PJMASKS

WHEELS OF A HERO!

Based on the episode "Wheels of a Hero!"

Ready-to-Read

Simon Spotlight
New York   London   Toronto   Sydney   New Delhi

SIMON SPOTLIGHT
An imprint of Simon & Schuster Children's Publishing Division
1230 Avenue of the Americas, New York, New York 10020
This Simon Spotlight edition December 2020
Adapted by May Nakamura from the series PJ Masks
This book is based on the TV series PJ Masks. All rights reserved,
including the right of reproduction in whole or in part in any form.
SIMON SPOTLIGHT, READY-TO-READ, and colophon are registered
trademarks of Simon & Schuster, Inc.
For information about special discounts for bulk purchases, please
contact Simon & Schuster Special Sales at 1-866-506-1949 or
business@simonandschuster.com.
Manufactured in the United States of America 1020 LAK
10 9 8 7 6 5 4 3 2 1
ISBN 978-1-5344-8056-8 (hc)
ISBN 978-1-5344-8055-1 (pbk)
ISBN 978-1-5344-8057-5 (eBook)

Greg, Connor, and Amaya
spot tracks on a wall.

Only the Gekko-Mobile
can drive up walls.
Someone must have
stolen it!
But who?

Connor becomes Catboy!

Greg becomes Gekko!

Amaya becomes Owlette!

They are the PJ Masks!

The PJ Masks look
for the Gekko-Mobile.

While they are looking, Armadylan steals the Cat-Car!

Night Ninja

has tricked Armadylan

into stealing all of

the vehicles.

Now he has

the Owl Glider too!

Night Ninja has also stolen
a special ninja medal.

It will make him
go super fast.

The vehicles can help him
take the medal
to Mystery Mountain.

Then he can unlock
the powers of the medal.

Night Ninja takes off!

He drives the Gekko-Mobile underwater.

He is too fast for Gekko.

Next, Night Ninja drives the Cat-Car through the city.

He is too fast for Catboy.

Then Night Ninja flies
in the Owl Glider.

He is getting closer
to Mystery Mountain!

"Sorry I helped Night Ninja steal your vehicles," Armadylan says.

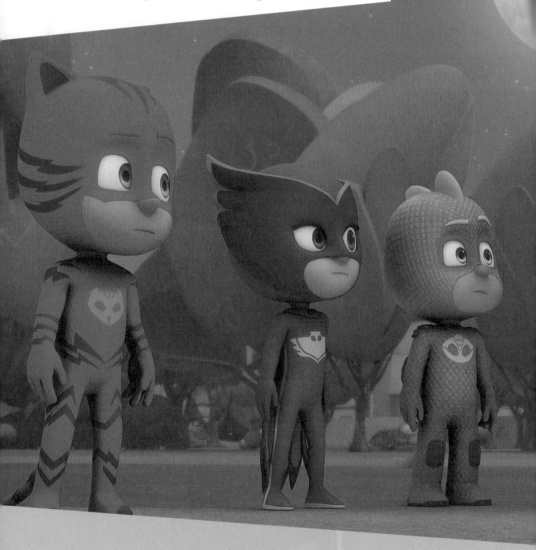

He has an idea.

Armadylan rolls
into a ball.
Gekko launches him
into the air!

Owlette uses
her Owl Wing Wind
to give him a boost.

Armadylan lands on
the Owl Glider.

He steers Night Ninja
away from
Mystery Mountain.

The PJ Masks
get their vehicles back
thanks to Armadylan
and *teamwork*!

"You are a real hero!"

Gekko tells Armadylan.

PJ Masks all shout hooray!

Because in the night

they saved the day!